Peppa Pig

Movie Night

Adapted by Cala Spinner

SCHOLASTIC INC.

Not sure how to say the word "night"?
Say it like this: n-eye-t, but put it all together: night!
You do not need to sound out the "g"!

ISBN 978-1-339-04953-3

10 9 8 7 6 5 4 3 2 1   24 25 26 27 28
Printed in the U.S.A.   40

First edition 2024
www.peppapig.com
Interior book design by Sophia La Torre

Peppa is going to
Penny Polar Bear's house.

It's movie night!

"We're going to watch the new Super Potato movie!" Penny says.

But first, Mummy Polar Bear
takes some pictures down.
The movie will be projected
on the wall.

The room gets dark.
Click! Click!

The projector shows a square
of light on the wall.
The room has turned into a
movie theater!

Everyone sits down.
Rebecca Rabbit is in front.

Her ears cast a shadow
on the screen.

That gives Penny an idea.
She uses her hands to make
a shadow bird.

Then Peppa makes a
shadow spider.

"Hee hee hee!" say Peppa's friends.

Rebecca and Suzy switch places.
Penny presses play on the remote.

The movie begins!

But then Penny stops the movie.
"We need snacks!" she says.

Mummy and Dr. Polar Bear
make popcorn.
Mummy Polar Bear likes
sweet popcorn.
Dr. Polar Bear likes
salty popcorn.

"I like sweet AND salty popcorn!" says Penny.

Peppa gets some popcorn, too.

When everyone has popcorn,
Penny presses play.
The movie begins again!

"I have seen this before!" says Pedro Pony. "In the end—"

"Shh!" the children say.
They do not want to
know the ending.

Onscreen, Mrs. Carrot loses a hat. "I lost a hat once!" says Rebecca.

"Oh no!" says Mandy Mouse.

"Shh!" say the children.

The movie starts again.
But now Danny has to
use the bathroom.

Peppa, Suzy, and
Gerald go, too.

Then Rebecca Rabbit asks
for a carrot.

Penny's mummies hand out carrots.

Penny presses play on the remote.

The movie begins again.

The children watch
the entire movie.

Mr. Potato saves the day.
Hooray!

What a fun night!

Peppa and her friends thank
Penny and her family for
inviting them over.

Peppa loves movie night.
Everyone loves movie night!